In lov
Henry Miller
died 12/27/86.
P9-BZB-901

"Goodbye Mom, Goodbye."

Philip E. Johnson

Illustrated by David Peacock

WELCH PUBLISHING COMPANY INC.
Burlington, Ontario, Canada

Sincere thanks to
Rudy and Ilona Kopriva
for their encouragement and support.

ISBN: 1-55011- 032-2

© 1987 by Philip E. Johnson

Welch Publishing Company Inc.
960 Gateway
Burlington, Ontario
L7L 5K7 Canada

All rights reserved. No part of this publication may be reproduced, stored in a retrieval system, or transmitted in any form or by any means without prior permission of the copyright owner.

Printed in Canada

DEDICATED TO MY MOTHER

"the best mom in the whole world"

Mary Ann Sawyer Johnson

Born in Halifax, Nova Scotia on December 5, 1908
Died in St. Thomas, Ontario on June 19, 1955

A PERSONAL NOTE TO THE READER

"Goodbye Mom, Goodbye" was written from my own experience. My mother died very suddenly when I was eleven years old. Unfortunately, even though I was loved very much, I was never really helped to grieve at that important time. More than a decade after her death, when I had dealt with my inner sadness, I decided to share with children my thoughts and feelings about life and death. I offer this book to you with the sincere belief that an understanding and appreciation of death is truly the beginning of life!

The Rev. Dr. Philip E. Johnson
Oakville, Ontario

"Hurry home from school," Mrs. Thompson called. "We want to pack the car so we can leave for the lake right after supper."

"Okay, Mom," replied Andrew as he and his sister Jennifer headed off to school. They turned at the corner to wave good-bye.

Andrew and Jennifer were really looking forward to the weekend. Their family always had a super time at the lake. During the afternoon Jennifer and Andrew must have looked at the classroom clock a hundred times. Finally the bell rang.

"Mom!" shouted Jennifer. "We're home!"

"I'm in the living room," Mr. Thompson called. Andrew and Jennifer looked at each other, surprised to hear his voice.

"Hi Dad! You're home early today," said Jennifer.

"Where's Mom?" Andrew asked.

"Jennifer and Andrew," said Mr. Thompson, "come and sit down with me. I've got something very important to talk to you about. This afternoon while your mom was busy getting things ready for the weekend, she had some really bad pains in her chest."

"Is she all right, Dad?" Jennifer enquired.

Mr. Thompson paused a long time before he answered.

"No. No, she's not. Mom phoned Dr. Edison, and she arranged right away for an ambulance to take Mom to the hospital."

Both Jennifer and Andrew snuggled in close to their dad, and he gave them both a hug.

Nobody said anything for a while. After a few moments, Andrew asked: "Can we go and see her?"

"Dr. Edison told me that it is most important that your mom rest quietly because she is very sick." said Mr. Thompson.

"I wish we could go and see Mom now!" said Jennifer.

"I know you do," Mr. Thompson agreed. "Perhaps tomorrow afternoon we could have a brief visit with her."

Friday evening, instead of watching the stars up at the lake, Jennifer and Andrew sat at their kitchen table. They thought a lot about their mom in the hospital. They decided to make her a gigantic get well card. On the outside Andrew drew a picture

of his mom. On the inside Jennifer printed a little note: "Sorry you're in the hospital, Mom. We miss you. Get well soon! Love, Andrew and Jennifer."

Mr. Thompson, Jennifer and Andrew went to the hospital on Saturday afternoon to visit Mrs. Thompson. The children could hardly wait to see their mom.

"Hi Mom," said Andrew softly. "This is for you."

"We made it ourselves," added Jennifer. "Andrew drew the picture of you on the front and I printed the words inside."

"Thank you," said Mrs. Thompson very quietly. "How thoughtful you are!" She opened the brightly coloured card and admired it for a moment. Then, drawing her children close to her, she whispered, "I miss you too."

She was very tired. After a brief visit, Jennifer and Andrew leaned over the big hospital bed and affectionately kissed their mom.

"Thanks for coming," Mrs. Thompson said. "Goodbye."

"Goodbye," echoed Jennifer and Andrew. "Goodbye."

At bedtime Jennifer and Andrew talked a long time with their dad about their mom's health. Mr. Thompson reassured them that Dr. Edison and the nurses at the hospital were doing everything they possibly could to help her. Then Mr. Thompson tucked his two children into their beds and kissed them good-night.

At five o'clock Sunday morning, the piercing ring of the telephone woke the family. Jennifer and Andrew heard their dad talking on the phone in their parents' bedroom. Then he hung up. They thought they heard their dad crying so they went to find out what was happening.

Mr. Thompson held his two children tightly as they sat on the end of the bed. Between sobs, he told them the terrible

news: during the night, Mrs. Thompson had had another heart attack, and had died.

They all cried for a long time. There was just no keeping back the big tears that rolled like waves over their cheeks. It must be a dream—a nightmare! It couldn't be true! It just couldn't be! They loved her so much. Now she was dead.

Mr. Thompson, Jennifer and Andrew felt numb all over.

Rev. Patterson, the minister of the church to which the Thompsons belonged, came to visit the Thompson family early Sunday morning. He hugged Mr. Thompson and the children and told them how sad he was about Mrs. Thompson's death. He asked their dad if the family would like him to lead them in a short prayer. Mr. Thompson nodded.

Rev. Patterson's prayer assured Mr. Thompson, Jennifer and Andrew of God's comfort and that God was with them during this very sad time.

For Andrew and Jennifer, that day seemed to be the longest day of their lives. They thought constantly about their mom. Things just wouldn't be the same without her. It was as if a part of them had died too.

They had a lot of confused feelings, mixed-up feelings, almost as if their insides had been turned upside-down. They felt very sad. They found themselves crying suddenly, right in the middle of washing dishes or answering the phone.

Jennifer and Andrew tried to think about the happy times they'd had with their mom. They remembered weekends at their cottage, things they might have been doing this weekend: splashing and swimming in the lake, playing ball, walking together along the beach, and listening to the rain pitter-patter on the cottage roof.

Andrew recalled her firmness with him when he did something wrong. He often got himself into trouble. But he remembered too how his mom comforted him when his grey-black squirrel Squeaker died. The two of them had a little funeral service for Squeaker and buried him in the corner of the backyard.

Jennifer remembered coming home from school on bitter cold afternoons when she and her mom had long friendly chats over hot chocolate, and ate peanut butter cookies fresh from the oven.

Jennifer and Andrew looked back on the birthday parties, Christmases and other wonderful celebrations their family had together. They both remembered how their mom had a special way of pulling them close to her warm body, wrapping them up in her arms and kissing them for no particular reason—just because she loved them!

On Sunday evening, Mr. Thompson sat down with Jennifer and Andrew to talk with them about the funeral arrangements. He explained that a funeral is a time to say goodbye to someone. People choose different ways of doing this. Some have a service in a church and some in a funeral home. Some choose to be buried. Some prefer to be cremated.

He and their mom had discussed what kind of funeral they would have if either of them died. In keeping with her own wishes, Mrs. Thompson's funeral service would be conducted at their church by Rev. Patterson on Tuesday afternoon, and Mrs. Thompson's body would be buried in the local cemetery.

The next day, their local newspaper carried an announcement of Mrs. Thompson's death.

Deaths

THOMPSON—At the General Hospital on Sunday, June 24, 1984, Sara Thompson in her 43rd year, of 67 West Street. Wife of Harold A. Thompson and mother of Jennifer and Andrew. Visiting at the McAlister Funeral Home on Monday from 2-4 p.m. and 7-9 p.m. Service at the First Avenue Church on Tuesday at 1.30 p.m.

On Monday afternoon, the Thompsons went to the McAlister Funeral Home. Jennifer and Andrew had often passed the red-brick building on the corner but they had never been inside. The funeral director, Mr. McAlister, a friendly man, greeted the Thompsons at the front door and led them into a room that looked like a living room. At the end of the room was a large, shiny wooden casket. Mr. Thompson, Jennifer and Andrew began to cry when they saw Mrs. Thompson's body in the casket. Mr. Thompson hugged Jennifer with one arm and Andrew with the other.

Nobody spoke for a long time.

During the afternoon, relatives and friends—some whom Jennifer and Andrew had never met before—visited the Thomp-

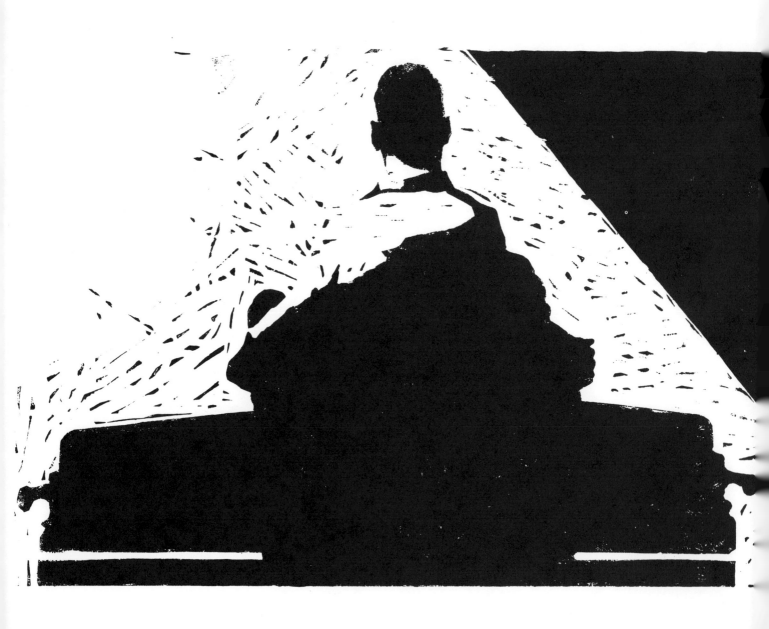

sons at the funeral home to say how sad they were that Mrs. Thompson had died. At times, the children felt they were drowning in words.

A few of Jennifer's and Andrew's friends from school came too. They didn't know what to say.

Some people sent beautiful flowers that were placed on both sides of the casket. Others gave money to a charity like The Heart Fund in memory of Mrs. Thompson.

Before they left, Mr. Thompson, Jennifer and Andrew placed on the casket a heart-shaped bouquet of deep red roses, Mrs. Thompson's favorite flower and colour. It was the Thompson family's way of saying "You're special. We love you."

Mrs. Thompson's funeral service was a simple and dignified ceremony. The people sang one of her favorite hymns. Rev. Patterson read from the Bible and talked about Mrs. Thompson's generous and loving life, her sudden death, and how very much she would be missed. He assured everyone—especially Mr. Thompson, Jennifer and Andrew—that God would comfort them at this very sad time.

At the end of the funeral service, six pall bearers, close friends of the Thompsons, carefully lifted Mrs. Thompson's casket, carried it outside and placed it in the funeral coach.

Jennifer and Andrew and their dad got into the car behind the funeral coach. They looked out the back window. Behind them, a long procession of cars drove with their headlights on. Each car had a little purple flag with "Funeral" printed on it waving in the breeze. It was like a parade for their mom!

When the people gathered at the graveside, Rev. Patterson said: "We commit Sara Thompson's body to the ground, earth to earth, ashes to ashes, dust to dust. Her body is gone but we shall always remember all she has meant to us all." Gazing through their tears, Jennifer and Andrew and their dad hugged each other.

"We love you, Mom," said Jennifer. "Goodbye."

Andrew swallowed the big lump in his throat and softly added, "Goodbye, Mom. Goodbye."

After the funeral, many relatives and friends dropped in at the Thompson's home for a reception. Andrew and Jennifer felt very lonely even though there were lots of people around them. They didn't feel very much like eating either. They felt numb. Was this really happening to them? Was it really their mother who had died? Was it just a bad dream, a nightmare?

When everyone had left, emptiness filled the house. For a long time the Thompsons sat silently in the living room, feeling very lonely. Suddenly Andrew, panic-stricken, blurted out: "You won't die, will you, Daddy? You won't leave us all alone? What will we do now? Who's going to be here when we come home at lunchtime or after school?"

"Who's going to take care of us?" asked Jennifer.

Mr. Thompson drew his two upset children to him. "I will *always* love you," he pledged earnestly. "*Always!*" He assured them that he was in good health, that their family would remain together and that all their needs would be taken care of.

"But why did *our* mom have to die? It's just not fair, Daddy!" Jennifer shouted.

"I've got lots of questions too, Jennifer," her father replied. "And I'm hurting inside. Sometimes life isn't fair and sometimes bad things do happen to good people. You see, it's important now for us to share with each other when we're sad or angry or confused or uncertain."

He hugged them closely, the way that Mom used to. "When your mom was in the hospital she asked me, if she died, to give each of you a couple of things of hers because you're so special.

"Jennifer, Mom wanted you to have her gold necklace you dreamed of wearing someday, and because you enjoy music so much, she wanted you to have her piano.

"And Andrew, Mom wanted you to have her camera, and because you like drawing pictures so much Mom thought you'd like to have her favorite painting in the front hall."

Andrew and Jennifer were pleased about the gifts, but they felt they shouldn't accept them. They kind of wanted to keep them for their mom in case she ever came back somehow.

For a couple of weeks Andrew and Jennifer found themselves thinking about their mother's death over and over. They couldn't think about anything else. They found it hard to concentrate in school. They would occasionally wake up at night with thoughts about their mother's death or about the uncertainty of the days ahead. Playing sports helped them to think about other things. Andrew played baseball and Jennifer played on the school soccer team.

Andrew and Jennifer's grandparents, their mom's mother and father, came to stay with them for three days while Mr. Thompson was away on a business trip. They had long chats. Their grandparents talked about their mom when she was just a little girl about their own age. It felt good to share their feelings of sadness.

Their grandfather said that people grieve in different ways, and that it takes some people longer than others to accept the death of someone they love—especially the death of a parent.

One Saturday afternoon Rev. Patterson called on the Thompsons and joined in playing catch with them in the back yard. After about ten minutes, Mr. Thompson suggested that they take a break and have a cold drink of lemonade on the patio.

"You took Mom's place today, Rev. Patterson," Andrew commented after his first glass of lemonade. "Mom always used to play four-corner catch with us."

"Your mother was a wonderful person, Andrew," said Rev. Patterson.

They gathered around the picnic table. They talked about how they were feeling now about their mom's death. The children asked Rev. Patterson lots of questions. He told them that he too had lots of unanswered questions about death. But he said it was very important to remember that God is love, and that no matter what happens to us, God is always with us!

In spite of their mom's death, life went on. Before they knew it, Jennifer and Andrew had finished school and were at the lake for the summer vacation with their dad. They missed their mom especially at the cottage. They were reminded of her in so many ways.

"Remember when Mom got down from the ladder last summer and got her foot stuck in the red water pail?" recalled Andrew.

"I remember when I got a privilege taken away from me because I was late. And it wasn't my fault! Mom had a bad temper sometimes," said Jennifer.

One day as they sat fishing off the dock at their cottage, Mr. Thompson pointed up to the clouds that hid the sun and said, "When your mom died it was as if the clouds drifted over us. But the clouds of sadness and hurt will pass in time and soon the sun will break through the clouds to light up our lives."

The fall, that year, was difficult for the Thompson family. Jennifer and Andrew missed what their mom had done to help them get ready for a new grade at school. In addition, they had to get used to a new person around their home, a housekeeper who was very kind but didn't do things quite the way their mom did. She didn't cook as well either.

The children thought about their mom often and chatted with their dad sometimes when they were alone. Sometimes they talked about it together. They recalled her most vividly on the first Christmas Day after her death. Christmas just wasn't the same without her! They missed her playing the Christmas carols while they gathered around the piano and the way she stuffed their Christmas stockings with all kinds of neat toys and treats. They missed their mother terribly.

From time to time during the winter, Andrew and Jennifer and their dad had moments of sadness and loneliness and anger. But these moments came less frequently. A couple of times, they started to cry for no obvious reason. Once the family went to the circus. First they laughed as they watched the clowns. Then they started to cry. Their mom had always especially enjoyed the clowns.

Almost a year after Mrs. Thompson's death, the Thompson family went back to the cemetery where she was buried. Jennifer and Andrew and their dad each gently placed a long-stemmed red rose on her grave. With tears in their eyes, they remembered what she meant to them.

Jennifer and Andrew still missed their mom. Once in a while

they felt confused and mixed up. Gradually the hurt they felt
deep inside went away, but not completely. Their mom had
died and life would never be the same again. Their love for her
would live on in their memories, precious memories of the most
special mom in the whole world!

"Goodbye Mom," they said. "Goodbye."